MOUSEBOAT

LARISSA THEULE
ILLUSTRATED BY ABIGAIL HALPIN

Viking

The wind is your voice.

You whisper to me.

Your chair is empty.

Your other chair, too.

The quilt you made smells like you.

Dad buys different laundry soap.
It doesn't smell like anything.

Dad does everything different.

The quiet is so loud.

I don't hear you at all in here.

But I know where I will.

THUNDER!

It was only a little, and far away.

Faye & Mama's Mouseboat

Please be out there.

YOU'RE HERE!

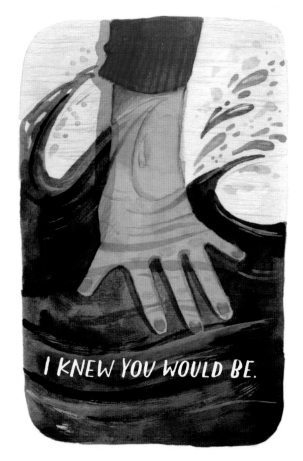

I KNEW YOU WOULD BE.

THE WAVES ARE YOUR VOICE.
Shhh, shhh, shhh.

IT'S NICE.

THE CLOUDS SWEEP IN FAST AND BRING ME SO MUCH MORE OF YOU.

NOW YOUR WORDS SURROUND ME

NOW I UNDERSTAND YOU.

Your voice carries me to shore.
I carry your words in my heart.

I am brave.

Faye & Mama's Mouse

I am home.

For my babies, Eero and Anya —L. T.
For Uncle Chris —A. H.

VIKING

An imprint of Penguin Random House LLC, New York

First published in the United States of America by Viking,
an imprint of Penguin Random House LLC, 2023

Text copyright © 2023 by Larissa Theule
Illustrations copyright © 2023 by Abigail Halpin

Visit us online at penguinrandomhouse.com.

Library of Congress Cataloging-in-Publication Data is available.

Manufactured in China

ISBN 9780593327357

1 3 5 7 9 10 8 6 4 2

TOPL

Design by Opal Roengchai
Text set in Hoefler Text
The illustrations in this book were created in watercolor, colored pencil, and digital.